For Mark, with love L.R.
For Laura, Grace and Oscar L.W.

First published in hardback in 2010 by Hodder Children's Books
First published in paperback in 2011
Text copyright © Lynne Rickards 2010
Illustration copyright © Lee Wildish 2010

Hodder Children's Books
338 Euston Road, London, NW1 3BH

Hodder Children's Books Australia
Level 17/207 Kent Street, Sydney, NSW 2000

The right of Lynne Rickards to be identified as the author and Lee Wildish
as the illustrator of this Work has been asserted by them in accordance with
the Copyright, Designs and Patents Act 1988.

ISBN: 978 0 340 98839 8
10 9 8 7 6 5 4

Printed in China

Hodder Children's Books is a division of Hachette Children's Books
An Hachette UK Company
www.hachette.co.uk

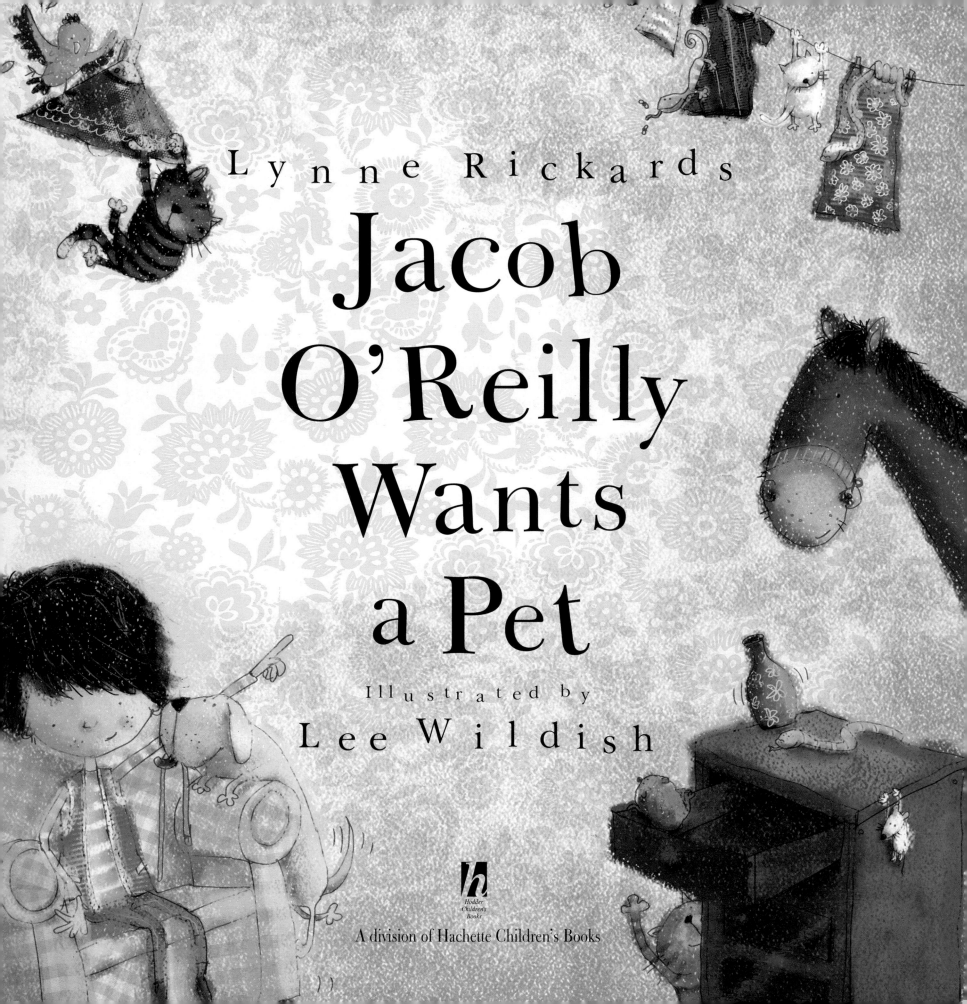

Lynne Rickards

Jacob O'Reilly Wants a Pet

Illustrated by

Lee Wildish

Hodder
Children's
Books

A division of Hachette Children's Books

Jacob O'Reilly had tried all he could
to convince Mum and Dad he'd be ever so good –
an absolute angel, the greatest son yet –
if only they'd let him have
one little pet!

He asked for a dog but Dad didn't want fleas.
He tried for a cat but the fur made Mum sneeze.

He went through a list of small rodents for sale,
but the very idea turned Mum and Dad pale.

'If I'm not allowed gerbils
or hamsters or mice,
don't you think an iguana
would be rather nice?

He'd be awfully quiet
and eat all the bugs,
and never leave fur or dead
birds on the rugs...

Oh, PLEASE can I have a pet?'

'An **emu** can make
a fine pet, have you heard?

It is said to be quite an affectionate bird,
and although it is tall and needs quite a large nest,
it keeps to itself and is never a pest...

Oh, **PLEASE** can I have a pet?'

'A walrus would be an ideal sort of pet.
He could live in the bathtub to keep himself wet.
I'd comb out his whiskers and scrub his broad back,
and brush those big tusks when he finished a snack...

Oh, PLEASE can I have a pet?'

Well, Mum and Dad thought about all these suggestions
while waiting for Jacob to run out of questions.

They pondered their choices and finally said,
'Why not try your own pet-sitting
business instead?'

The very next day, Jacob put up a sign:
'Come one and come all! Any number is fine!
I'll care for your pets while you take a nice break.
They'll have a great time here with
Pet-Sitter Jake!'

In no time at all Jacob had a full house –
four **dogs** and
five **hamsters**,
six **cats** and one
mouse...

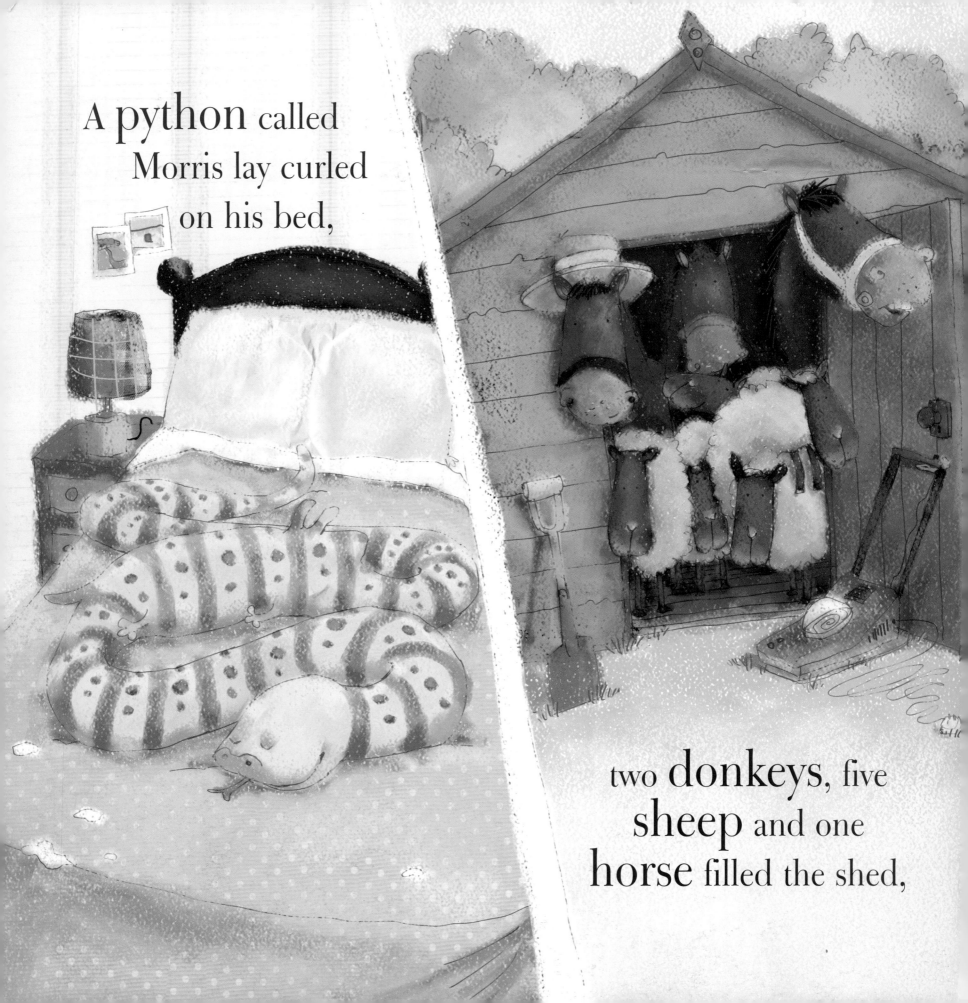

A python called
Morris lay curled
on his bed,

two donkeys, five
sheep and one
horse filled the shed,

the kitchen was hopping
with **rabbits** and **hares**,

and somebody's zebra
was blocking the stairs.

At feeding time Jacob was run off his feet –
some pets wanted salad, and some wanted meat.
They needed a hose-down when dinner was done,
and then it was time for a marathon run!

When two weeks were up and the owners came back,
The house had turned into a flea-bitten shack.
The minute the last pet whizzed off into town,
Pet-Sitter Jake went and pulled his sign down!

And that's when he noticed a rather fine snail,
Just sitting contentedly there on a nail.
'Hello, there,' smiled Jacob, 'I don't think we've met.'
And finally Jacob had found the right pet!

Other great Hodder picture books perfect to share with children:

978 0 340 95711 0

978 0 340 98868 8

978 0 340 98866 4

978 0 340 98805 3

978 0 340 96000 4

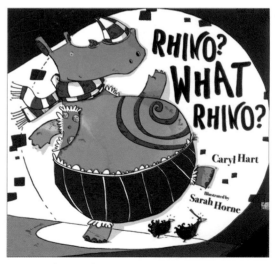

978 0 340 98140 5